the forsaken...

the forsaken...

Chad V. Broughman

Etchings Press

Indianapolis

This publication is made possible by funding provided by the Shaheen College of Arts and Sciences and the English Department of the University of Indianapolis. Special thanks to IngramSpark and to those students who judged, edited, designed, and published this chapbook: Kylie Seitz and Zach Meadows.

UNIVERSITY *of*
INDIANAPOLIS

Published by Etchings Press
1400 E. Hanna Ave
Indianapolis, Indiana 46227

etchings.uindy.edu
www.uindy.edu/cas/english

Printed by IngramSpark
www.ingramspark.com

Printed in the United States of America

ISBN-13: 978-0-9988976-1-5

23 22 21 20 19 18   2 3 4
Second Printing, 2019

dedication

---

for my sons,

Gray and Hudson

table of contents

the day the guinea pigs went missing

The night of the lawyer's visit, Ma took a thrashing, and the next morning, Pa holed up in the garage. From dawn to dusk, he toiled away, the sounds of hard work and carpentry banging through the solitary window, and my brothers and I perched beneath it, waiting. For what, we didn't know. But that did not stop us from wild speculation. Samuel said, "I think it's a roller coaster this time. A big one. With loops."

"No way," I said. "The garage ain't big enough—"

"Is too," he said.

"It's gonna have giant loops, upside down ones."

"Maybe, little brother," Glen said. Then he turned to me and put a finger against his lips, an arm around my neck. "But I hope it's a boat," he said. "We'll sail across Lake Huron and leave Michigan forever." He pointed north as if he could see Canada, and Samuel and I knew to stay quiet, to give him the moment. I remember that the thought made my heart feel jerky and my stomach empty and light. It was thrill, not fear, at the notion of disappearing.

The sun had dipped by the time Pa came out, and there were broken breezes coming off Lake Michigan, cooling our wet skin. His arms were spanned wide as an albatross and in them was a custom-built tilt-table. It was the grandest thing I'd ever seen. Smooth cedar, reddish brown, and long, spindly legs that thinned out into wide camel feet. We followed him close as he headed toward the house. He set it down on our slanted porch and bent his neck, measuring the severity of its lean, then went back to the garage. We approached with caution, none of us daring enough to touch it but too anxious not to peek at its sleek top. A perfectly mapped maze with dark, dotted lines. And to help guide the ball past the round, black holes, there were little raised ridges glued just so. "For you, Samuel," Pa said, returning with a few shims in tow. "See, high walls and a big knob. You can play one-handed." We gathered around while Pa stacked tiny wood pieces beneath the two farthest legs. After it was balanced, he pushed Samuel in front and pulled a heavy silver ball from the pocket of his overalls. He dropped it—a low clunk—and it sat completely still. "Yep," he said. The table was more magnificent than all our guesses.

Ma watched from the kitchen. Amidst our laughter and yucking, I saw Pa motion to her with his head. He pulled back his shoulders and nodded toward the table with a proud smile, most of his teeth showing. But Ma put a palm over her black eye, waited till we were all looking at her, then drew the curtains closed.

Samuel was born without a hand. "Because of goddamn Vietnam," Pa always said. And that's why he had tried to seek justice from the powers-that-be. "Agent fuckin' Orange!" he barked at the attorney. "And whaddya mean I 'can't sue the government'?" Pa taunted the slight man, poking his chest and rearing up his fifth of gin. "Why the hell not? You know, it's 'cause of us leathernecks that you even got to be a fancy lawyer!" Then he circled around him and said, "All dressed up like some kinda ice cream cone." We all silently prayed for the man to keep his mouth shut. He did. And we got a new tilt-table.

Our house was old with spare walls and worn wood floors that echoed my parent's words, their fisticuffs, and their temperaments: my father, bold and staunch, and my mother, yielding and deliberate. We heard all their fights, but Pa's voice boomed—"Just trying to talk to you 'bout how I'm feeling, that's all."—and Ma's was level and antagonizing—"Then talk," she'd say. Always, my older brother Glen would tell us to plug our ears and think of something nice. It was the day-afters, as we came to call them, when Pa's true heart shone, though. At least, I like to think so.

A day-after also meant that Pa would start eating dinner with us for a while. Eventually though, he'd skip a night, and Ma would say something like, "Well, one day, maybe I'll get to have nice things."

Then, Pa would harden, skip another night. Before too long, we would hear his angst bouncing off the walls again: "You're always acting sad, making the boys feel bad for you. Looking for pity, all the damn time. And don't tell me no beating from a nun did that."

"Sorry," Ma would whisper, and in my mind, I could see her eyes rolling.

It was in the thistle of their heart-to-hearts that I pieced together the clues to Ma's need for attention, her strange antics. See, between the bouts of uproar—the calm before the storm, Glen called it—I'd spend time in town, didn't want to be at home when the rat's nest opened up. At the end of Main Street was the only tall building in Beaumont, our church. Though the chapel was wide and boxy, the spire was thin and came to a point. On top, a cross, white and sturdy. I often wondered how it always looked so new, even though it endured Michigan's brutal winters, year after year. Yet through the ice and sleet and gale winds, there it stood, unperturbed. Behind, in its shadow, was the Beaumont Academy for Girls, or the slaughter house as the locals called it, an abandoned boarding school. It had closed in the mid-60's due to pressure from the suits in Lansing (I'd later find out in high school). But in my elementary years, the neglect had already taken a toll. Some of the windows had been busted out, and those that weren't were cracked, splintering out like a dragon tree. The mortar had given way in spots, so the bricks were crumbling, red and gray. I used to think it looked like red velvet cake, but I knew from all the rumors that nothing sweet could ever stem from such a place. That's what added to the rush of climbing up the wobbly fire escape on the back side and sitting in the emptiness, knowing that what happened within those walls was so horrific that people just walked away, leaving everything behind, even dirty plates and half written notes, mid-sentence.

The winds had scattered papers across the floor—yellowed but intact—and on the ceiling, the paint had peeled and puckered, scab-like. Taking a glimpse over the wrap-around railing, I could see that the lower level was a hostel for rodents, so I stayed up top, where someone had pushed the desks and chairs against the walls. The bookshelves had been brought out into the big open space in the center, still holding dozens of hardcovers. That's where I sat, in a gap between two shelves. Over the archway in front of me, carved in perfect cursive, were the words, "To be great is to be misunderstood." Under that, to the right, someone had spray painted a wide brown fist, the words "Fuck Life" and "Suck Me" on either side. Pockets of spider webs clung tight to the fancy crown molding but had given way in other places. The thin, fragile strands dangled free and when the sun's rays slanted just so, they lit up, some pale, some silver.

I remember that first morning, when my friend unfastened the shackle on the padlock and pushed open the big wood door with ease. I can still see the frantic robin that couldn't find its way out, slamming against the walls, over and over, till its head split open. With each thrash, another tiny blot of blood. A sense of relief washed over me when it finally thudded to the floor and in the dust and grime, lay quiet. Then I thought about the orphans, all the stories. How late one night, trying to escape, a girl toppled out the window and sat on the sidewalk below, her broken legs bent beneath her, too afraid to cry out. Or the girls who vomited into their bowls of cold oatmeal—blackened with crawling weevils—were forced to eat that, too. And the skinny nun with a moustache who erased the chalkboard with the girls' hair or their faces if they made a mistake. I heard about a few women around town with marred cheeks and bare spots on their scalps. Actually, it was that detail that gave away Ma's secret. One night, when Pa was still out, she was brushing her hair in front of the bathroom mirror, and I saw the hairless patch on her scalp. She held a clump of curls in one hand

and stared hard at the stark place for a long time, oblivious to everything around her, including me.

Then, there was the stormy Saturday morning we lost power, and Pa took us all to breakfast at Irma's Diner. The memory stays with me for several reasons. First, it was the only time I can recall eating at a restaurant as a family. But what's more, when the waitress brought Pa's oatmeal, Ma clamped her hands over her mouth, gagging as she ran from the table. While Glen and Samuel laughed, I sat dumbstruck, convinced of her foundling past. And the most unexpected thing was Pa defending Ma, to the best of his ability: "Shut up, boys," he said. "It ain't funny."

Then, in '81, the ultimate day-after hit. It was mid-July, just after my eleventh birthday, and Pa bellowed our names from the front yard. We flew down the stairs, tackling one another to get there first. He nodded to his dull red Chevy. I remember the middle panels, mushroom-white, and Samuel always saying that it looked like a bowl of berries and butter. The three of us clamored aboard, scooting across the sticky beige pleather. Our sweaty legs made fart noises; even Pa chuckled, cloudy though he was.

"Where to, Pa?" Samuel asked.

"Mr. Pratt's farm," he said, groggy but pleasant.

We all knew that Mr. Pratt raised guinea pigs, yet we didn't understand the magnitude of this day-after gift, at least not right away. We looked to Pa for more explanation. His mouth was bunched to one side, like when someone is trying to make you laugh but you'll get in trouble if you do, and his eyes were tired but glistening. I came to the realization first. "You mean, we're getting some?"

Pa's nod was slight but undeniable. When Ma stepped onto the porch, his smile died. He held down the brake, hammered the gas, then let go. Our necks jolted backward and gravel sprayed against the house. He shouted over the tumult, "That oughta rile up your Ma! Get her some pity from the neighbor lady! She'll love that!" He thrust up his middle finger and held it out the window. I peered into the rearview mirror and watched her walking along the dense, brick-hued Barberry bushes that separated our house from ol' Ms. Atkin's place. As Ma neared the end of the row, she slowed down, then stood in the patch of wild, waist-high thimbleweed on the edge of the property line. She pulled a silky yellow bandana from her loose ponytail, letting her thick brown tresses fall around her shoulders, and I thought about the stark space above her ear, how well she hid it. Just before we turned onto Summit Street, out of view, I could see her body heaving. She sucked in real hard—her chest lifting and falling—working herself into a frenzy. Then she bent over and mussed up her hair with both hands. And I swear I saw her start limping.

"Whatcha gonna name yours?" Glen asked. He was a sullen boy, but with big events, like Christmas or Ma's beatings or this, he always tried to act paternal, even though it sounded clumsy.

"I dunno."

"I'm calling mine Juliet." With his splayed-out fingers, he tried to grip my head like a basketball as Pa always did, but his hand was too small.

The sign was penned in big, block letters—GUINEA PIGS—across a piece of cardboard, taped to a leaning stake. The deeper we drove into the Pratt farm, the louder the rodents' chattering grew, eventually swelling into an all-out furor. My brothers ran off as soon as the truck stopped, beckoning me from different places: "Look at that one!" and "Come see this one!"

I stayed by Pa and Mr. Pratt, hoping they would guide me to the perfect pup. Already, Pa had said things like, "He's a stout son of a gun, ain't he?" and "Now there's a glossy coat, and no cowlicks."

Eventually, Mr. Pratt led me to a far corner, telling me how he painted all the cages different colors. "That way, I can keep track of them better, group them by age, or breed or—"

"Why is this cage red?" I asked.

He laughed. "Well, Mrs. Pratt calls these pups the trouble makers. The spunky ones, she says. I thought red might fit. Don't you think?" By then, I had already spotted a likely contender. She was gamboling by a mound of wood chips, but here and there, she peeked out from behind it, holding my gaze for a few seconds. Against her caramel-colored coat, her inky eyes looked like punctuation marks. "Ah. You've spotted Lucy." She twitched her ears, barely visible beneath her shaggy fur, and crinkled her spongy, pink nose.

"Lucy?"

"Yep. See, I was painting the cage one afternoon, and the little bugger got excited. She hopped in the air, pretty darn high, too. 'Popcorning,' it's called. Anyway, I tipped my paint can some, and she became a redhead."

"I Love Lucy," Pa said. Mr. Pratt winked. I swooped her up in my hands, looking for the red spots, but there weren't any left. The name stuck, though. I was smitten.

Several day-afters later, when the novelty of the tilt-table had passed, Pa burrowed himself in the garage again. When he surfaced this time, the table was a magnificent hutch for our woolly rodents, complete with several different rooms and a water dispenser. Besides, Samuel could never angle the silver ball through that maze—that's why, just for fun, we named his pig Lucky. Pa didn't hit Ma that night. Though Glen and Samuel had fallen asleep, I heard Pa say to her, "Thought about you, seeing them critters caged up like that." Ma let his words hang, and I could feel Pa's humiliation through the wall, curdling the air. After a minute or two, he broke the silence. "I'm going to sleep in the garage, don't wanna fight." I heard him shuffle to their door, then pause before saying, "Feels like getting mercy's more important to you than—" A hush followed. Though I know better than to think Pa cried, I'm certain that he must have come close, at least close enough for me to realize there was some kind of love there. "Thinkin' that place might'a broke you," he finally said. I heard the door shut then Pa making his way down the hall.

That morning, Ma wore her bulky, gray turtleneck anyway, the one she always wore if Pa put marks on her.

"But you ain't hurt. Why you wearing that?" Glen asked.

"Am too," Ma said. "Mind your business." It wasn't much longer before ol' Ms. Atkins came to the door. Standing with her was Mrs. Riley, the lady from church who always wore big, flowery hats and snapped her gum.

"Welcome. Glad you agreed to tea." Ma ushered them in and shooed us out. After a couple of hours, we came back in for water and some snacks and heard Ma saying, "It's already turning purple. I wear this heavy shirt, so the boys can't see." When we peered into the living room, she was holding herself in a hug, her head hung low. Glen stormed back outside. But I stood still, thinking things through some. I was mad at Pa. Why did he even hit her at all? I was disgusted, too, on account of Ma tricking these women. I recall a little guilt for feeling that way, knowing she'd spent time in the slaughter house and thinking of all the nice things she did, like always cleaning up after us, making supper every night and helping clean our fish—if we caught any—always saying she didn't mind even though we knew she hated it.

Like the time we came home from the grocery and there were extra bags because it was the 4th of July. Potato chips and sparklers, stuff like that. Trips to the A&P were hard on her. We could only afford to go once a week, and she was always busting at the seams with coupons, hiding them in the pockets of her little brown purse—the canvas one, with rows of dangling tassels, looked like a horse's mane. She called it her fancy handbag, and when I asked her why she took it to the A&P, she said, "All the women in town will be judging us," and swept her checkered skirt with both hands. "What's really sad, Clint, is that I care."

I never told her about the time I saw Mrs. Morris and her fat friend Mrs. Bilodeau pointing at her that Thanksgiving as we headed to the checkout lane. One of them, not sure which, said, "What's she carrying, a saddlebag?" and the other cackled like a hyena. When they looked my way, I lurched at them, even growled some. They both ducked down the Health and Beauty aisle.

Per usual, Ma had gotten out of the car, a bag in each arm. Glen and I had done the same. Samuel had hopped out and was heading toward the woods.

"Whoa, young man. There's more bags this time. Bring some in, please."

"I can't," Samuel said. "I only have one hand, remember?" There was a moment of stillness before the whirlwind of tough love and spitfire. Nothing dared move, not even the air. Ma turned slow and steady, let loose her bags. They struck the ground at the same time, making an awkward thump. I watched the bottoms of them start to darken with the broken-open contents, rather than look at her, or Glen, or Samuel especially.

"You will carry those bags, sir," she said, then pointed to the car, "and all the rest of them, too!" I'd never heard her shout before—she was always prodding Pa in a hushed sort of way—and her high-pitched tone made my bladder twinge. "Put those bags down, boys," she said, her voice still charged. "Samuel's gonna get them." As Glen and I set down our wares, I peeked at Ma and my little brother. Hands on her hips, their noses almost touching. The fancy horse-purse had swung to the front of her and was swaying between them like a pendulum. I quickly refocused on the sullied bags, which were starting to wilt. I don't know how much time ticked by before I heard Ma patter across the driveway, but I bowed my head as she passed, watched the heels of her olive-colored plastic shoes kick up dust.

"Two minutes, Samuel," she said over her shoulder. "Not a second more."

I could hear my little brother sniveling and the paper bags crinkling as he picked them up. I thought Ma heartless. After I thought a safe amount of time went by, I bee-lined for the bathroom to relieve my angst. Ma was already in there, though, and the door was locked. Behind it, I heard her crying. Not the fake kind like when she wanted us to hate Pa but real weeping, like her guts were pulling apart.

Juliet and Lucky and Lucy, they became our world. We held them for hours at a time, watched them groom one another, and listened to the wheeking and whining. We overfed them, too—only the most tender alfalfa would do. Pa said to make sure the seeds were bright yellow and the pods dark brown, so we handpicked their meals from the field behind the school, and after the harvest had ended, we stole hay from the 4H building. Glen and I did our semester essays on the history of guinea pigs. He got an A, and me, a B+. My teacher wrote, "Great essay, Clint. Watch your spelling," and Samuel took Lucky to show and tell. Our pigs gave us dignity. We weren't used to feeling that. What's more, we never grappled over whose pup was better. In our heart of hearts, we just knew that our own pup was the best. An unspoken truth.

Until Lucy started attacking the others.

"How're the vermin, son?" Pa asked one night, swaying and clutching the counter.

"Great, Pa," we said.

He tousled our hair and stumbled away, sneering at Ma, then said, not so softly, "I win." As the night rolled on, their tones grew snarkier. One at a time, each of us found our way to the tilt-table cage. We stroked our pups in silence, waiting for the bickering to start. That's when Samuel noticed the blood on Lucky's ear. Then Juliet's.

Turns out that Lucy was a dominator. The "head honcho," Mr. Pratt called her when we trekked the four miles to his farm with our guinea pigs in tow.

"So she hurts them on purpose?" I asked. My voice started to quiver, and I was afraid that I wouldn't be able to stop the tears that had formed behind my eyes.

"Sorry, son. Lucy probably butts them with her head. And jumps at 'em, too. I'm sure you've seen her mount the others, right?" We had, but we usually just giggled, made wisecracks, even imitated them. Never thinking much of it. "Look, boys, it's natural. It's what they do. Hell, it's what people do, too. In our own way."

"Will she ever stop?" My tone was pleading, and I knew it. But at that point, I didn't care anymore. Glen slipped his hand over mine.

"She ain't gonna kill the others, Clint," Mr. Pratt said. "Just wants to let 'em know that she's in charge, that's all. Now go home, boys. Play with 'em like you always do. They're the same ol' sows."

For the first mile, we walked in silence. Samuel lagged, holding Lucky tight, already forgetting why we'd come in the first place—sometimes it slipped my mind that Samuel was three years younger than me. Glen spoke first, "I ain't mad at you."

"Okay." Then I said, "Don't know if I want her anymore."

"Don't talk that way, Clint."

"It's true. I don't want a bully pup!" And I began to cry.

So, when Lucy started sneezing all the time, I only pretended to be upset. I knew that Glen and Samuel cared much more than I did. Pa told us her eyes were milky because there were pieces of hay stuck in them. "It's 'cause she's a fast eater," he said. "Always trying to get hers first." He chuckled. Not me, though. I was embarrassed of her. When she died the following week from pneumonia, I buried her in the thimbleweed between ol' Ms. Atkins' yard and ours. Then I ran into town, climbed up the rickety ladder, and burrowed between the shelves, listening for echoes of the tortured girls. Their pain was worse than mine, I thought, and there was comfort in that.

Not long after, on a nimble autumn day, cloudless and crisp and blue, we raced home from school, Glen and Samuel wanting to feed their blithesome pigs and me wanting to visit the slaughter house before dark.

"Ma! Where's Juliet?" Glen's voice cracked. The tilt-table hutch was empty. Ma stood at the sink, hands busy with suds and dishes. Her back to us.

"Ask your father," she said. Pa was nowhere to be found, but of course, that was her point. I think. No matter how much begging, the response was always the same, "Ask your father," and when Pa finally did come home, he had none to give.

"You boys have any friends over?" he asked. "Maybe they was stolen." Then he turned to Ma and raised his shoulders. "I just don't get it, do you?" She said nothing.

For a while, my brothers asked every day. I helped them search everywhere. In the yard, the woods, the fields. We listened hard to Ma and Pa fighting, hoping for clues. "Where are they?" Pa would roar, and in return, Ma would say gingerly, "I don't know."

Glen changed the day the pigs went missing. His face turned downward, and he didn't bother trying to be kind or fatherly anymore. He didn't bother with much of anything. Samuel questioned their whereabouts a few times, asked if animals went to Heaven once, but was easily diverted with candy or a tickle under his arm. Otherwise, we never spoke of our guinea pigs again.

That winter was brutal—blustery, gray and full of second-rate day-afters. But one in particular left scars, the kind you can see. Early on a Sunday morning, we were corralled into Pa's ol' Chevy for a trip to the sledding hill over in Montcalm County. Ma had objected, talking about the Sabbath. But Pa simply replied, "Not today," then under his stale breath, he called her pious and a bitch.

"I'm going too," Ma said and climbed into the truck before Pa could stop her. When he bumbled to the garage for another sled, she turned to us with a pinched face and darting eyes. "Be careful, boys," she said, "He's still drunk." There was fear in her voice. We felt it.

"I don't want to go," Samuel said.

"Me neither," she replied. Though we knew she couldn't protect us, her trying to felt good.

At first, skidding on the black ice felt like going down a big slide, a free fall. But then, Pa jerked the steering wheel. Hard right. We drifted sideways, and Ma's shriek split the dead air. The truck crashed into a grove of snow-leaden pines, and there was a ringing in my ears—a thin, constant thrum that lasted several days. For the most part, Pa, Samuel and I were unscathed, but not Ma. She bruised her nose against the dashboard. And surely not Glen. Two glass shards had struck his face, cutting open his cheek and lancing an eye. Though the doctor saved his sight, the wounds were jagged and ugly. The following week, Pa overheard Ma on the phone lying to her sister. "He broke my nose," she said. So later, with an open palm, he did. That day-after's offering was a chocolate Lab puppy named Hershey. When it yipped, Pa kicked it, and if it begged, he threw it against the wall. By February, the pup ran away. We were all happy for him. But it was in May when our world caught fire.

Glen burst into the house holding a burlap sack, both of them dripping onto the linoleum floor. Ma stood behind the open refrigerator. "You been swimming in that dirty crick again?" Glen said nothing, his lips thin and pale. "I asked you if you've—" She peered around the door as she spoke. A jar of beets fell from her grasp and cracked open. The peppery, pungent smell flooded the room. They glared at one another. Then Ma stepped over the red juice and broken glass, her arms open.

"Don't." My brother held up his hand and cocked his

head, staying fixed on her face. He wiped at his eyes. When he threw down the bag, rocks and tiny bones spilled at our feet. "I think you lost this," he said, and his voice was strong. He pulled her muddy yellow scarf from his pocket, tossed it onto the grisly pile. "What did they ever do to you?" he cried out, then skulked back through the door.

Ma moved to me next, put her arms around my waist and whispered, "Sorry." There was no visible damage this time, only sadness, like when I watched her drinking tea with Ms. Atkins and the ladies from church. I thought about telling Glen that day about Ma and the slaughter house. But then I wondered if he might already know. What if he had found out about her boarding school days, too? What if someone had told him about the girls' screaming—tied to their iron beds and locked in cages—yet it didn't matter? Maybe for Glen, nothing would ever justify Ma's foul deeds.

The space between that fateful spring and the death of my Pa was wide but ordinary. I'm sure there were a few joyful times and many more domestic battles, yet none come to mind. My brothers and I survived, even flourished in some ways: Samuel with his college degree and Glen and I with families of our own. We were men when Pa died. It was a misty Wednesday morning, and the sky was drab. At the funeral, Ma cried, but when we drove her back home, she called him a 'sonofabitch.' And I said, "I loved him." With that, she turned on her heel.

"Why?" she hissed.

After that, our relationship is cool at best. We manage to putter through holidays and births and deaths and such, but when Glen brings his kids over so all the cousins can play, we don't invite Ma. Sometimes, as I'm talking to Glen, I can't help staring at his eye, the rust-colored stain on his cornea plain-as-day. He knows I'm looking because he'll say, "Think of something nice, little bro." Then we'll see Samuel running in circles with his nieces and nephews, rubbing his stump and howling like a child himself. We laugh. There are moments I regret not asking Ma about her past, but fewer with each passing year. I figure if certain childhood questions aren't asked by adulthood, they can only cause pain. The other day, I caught a glimpse of Juliet in my mind's eye. She was grazing on a cool, grassy plain, Lucky and Lucy by her side.

Uriah's last rite

At first, no one gave it much thought, not even Uriah's father, Mr. Lovett. He just figured all kids were a bit delicate, both girls and boys. But the day Uriah turned eleven, his ways were too gentle for 1857, especially in northern Michigan. The kids' teacher, Miss Kauffman, prompted them to sing Happy Birthday, and after, she turned to Uriah and said, "It's your special day. You choose recess."

Uriah fixed his eyes on a widening hole in the toe of his boot, hovered his other boot over it.

"Well? What will it be?"

Uriah anguished. *Just say stickball*, he thought, *like you're supposed to*. His heart loped. Skin turned clammy. He thought, *No*, and wrestled within. *Tell the truth. Be a man.* Before he could talk himself down, he uttered, "Can we read more from *Walden* or *The Scarlet Letter*?"

Miss Kauffman's face appeared strained, like she was puzzled but wanted to look approving. "Certainly, Uriah," she said. With her foot, she quietly nudged the bag of balls and bats back under her desk. All the kids groaned, boys louder than girls, deriding Uriah under their breaths. Miss Kauffman shushed them, waved her knobby hand in a stopping motion, then gave them a teacher look—narrow eyes, scrunched up face. That week after Sunday services, she tugged on Mr. Lovett's shirt. Uriah picked up on the hint from her uncomfortable glance. They needed privacy. He walked ahead of them but curiosity overshadowed prudence, and he ducked behind the archway, out of sight, not out of earshot.

"The boys are calling him an odd-stick," Miss Kauffman said, "really giving him a go."

"Any of 'em clean his plow yet?"

"Almost. I tell them to skedaddle, but the truth is, sir, if they ever set their minds to beating the boy, I couldn't stop them."

"Callin' him soft, I s'pose?" Mr. Lovett spoke in a hushed voice.

"Yes, that's the whole of it."

Uriah's heart pounded hard. He took a quick peek around the doorway to see his father rubbing his stubbly chin while Miss Kauffman picked at the hem of her skirt. He heard all the "howdy-do's" as the God fearing folks of Beaumont shuffled past, out into the morning shine. Then, just the three of them were left alone in the chapel, except for Father Hiram, still standing at the pulpit, gathering up the loose pages of his tattered bible.

In a dragging lull, Uriah's father spoke again, "Think I'll keep him home this harvest, ma'am. Let things simmer down some."

"Oh, but Mr. Lovett, he's a bright boy, sir. I don't think—"

"Ain't your place, ma'am. This here's a family matter."

Uriah knew the reason why, but he asked anyway. "Pa, I never stayed home for harvest before." His voice cracked. "How come now?" A glimmer of hope flashed through him.

Maybe I'd misunderstood. That's it. I'm not a sissy. There's word in town of an early winter. That's why he's pulling me from school.

"'Cause I said, boy." The glimmer died instantly.

Uriah's hiatus started the next day. His mother woke him early. "Get dressed. Your Pa's waiting for you in the barn." Uriah could feel her awkwardness. *Look into my face, Ma,* he thought. *You'll see, I don't blame you.* She kept her eyes fixed, just above his head.

"Hurry up, child. Breakfast is getting cold. You know how he gets." She stepped to the door and paused. After a deep breath, she turned to Uriah, tilted her head, poised to speak. But she said nothing, just gave half a smile.

"What is it, Ma?"

She shook her head back and forth. "You make your Pa proud out there," she said, then stepped through the door and pulled it closed. For a long while, she stood on the other side. Uriah watched her silhouette through the thin gap between the floor and the bottom of the door. Then she slipped away, like a mouse changing course, the shadow replaced by the yellow slant of dawn.

After dressing, Uriah scurried to the kitchen and sat at the table alone, a plate of bacon and eggs and steaming grits awaiting him. He scooped up a heap of grits and dabbed them into the orange yolk, then raised it to his mouth.

"Boy! Bring my rifle, quick!" Uriah dropped the spoon mid-air and ran to the corner of the loft where the rifle leaned against the wall. He hated guns. When he was five, Grandpa Lovett had called him to the stables to watch him shoot a lame colt. He said, "You need to know about these things." Uriah watched as his Grandpa traced an imaginary X with his finger, from the horse's left ear to right eye, then right ear to left eye, and placed the barrel just above the intersection. The rifle thumped a bullet into the colt's skull, but it didn't die. It fell to the ground and scoured its good legs against the gravel, trying to stand up, trying to live. Uriah turned to run, but his Grandpa shouted, "Get back here, son!" then reloaded and shot the colt again. It grunted several times then seized, hard and slow, like cooling molasses.

Now, though, Uriah's concern for his father outweighed his fear. He grabbed the rifle and the small wood box next to it. It was a Kentucky Flintlock, slender as a finger and glossy from years of his father's diligent, attentive polishing. He held it away from his body in upturned palms, as if it were made of glass, then stepped lightly but hastily outside. Mr. Lovett was standing in front of the henhouse, hands on his broad, bulky hips, looking in, scratching the back of his head. The chickens bawked wildly, shuffling about the pen, their rumpled feathers wafting through the open wire fence up top. Without looking Uriah's way, he said, "That you, son?"

"Yes, sir."

Taking a step back, Uriah's father kept his head toward the coop but glanced at him. "Boy, you're holding that gun like it'll bite you," he said. "We gotta coon in there. If it's out in daylight, it's prob'ly rabid."

Uriah's breath began to quicken, and his belly fluttered. *Don't make me do this.* His father took the rifle and set its stock on the ground with the barrel pointing skyward. He pulled a dented red tin from the wood box and poured the black grainy powder into the muzzle. Uriah watched his father's deep concentration with mixed emotion—fear, respect, and a bit of hatred—his father's fat, pink tongue peeking from the corner of his mouth.

"Pa, I can't shoot. Best if you do it."

His father said nothing, just stuffed the metal ball into the barrel and reached for the ramrod. Then his face slackened. "Where's the start rod, boy?" Uriah played dumb and looked around, too, knowing he'd forgotten it. His father mumbled under his breath and searched for a stick, then plunged the ammunition down the rifle's tube. Then he set the flintlock and shoved the piece into Uriah's hands. The emotions tipped, less respect, more fear and hatred.

"Pa, I can't—"

"'Bout damn time you tried, boy. Hear that rascal hissing? You want it killin' the whole damn flock? Now, I'll roil it out of there, then you blast him." He walked backward to the side of the coop. "Set her at half cock," he coached, "and step back some."

Uriah raised the gun, unwieldy in his grip. "Pa?"

"That's it. Now push her against your shoulder. Focus." Uriah's father lifted his arms above his head, angled them toward the henhouse. Uriah thought he looked like a criminal under arrest. "Ready?" he yelled.

No, Uriah screamed inside, and his hands shook violently. Then he lowered the barrel.

"Take aim, boy!'"

Uriah raised the gun again and cried out, "I can't do this!"

His father slammed his fists against the wobbly coop, beating it like a drum, and whooped, fierce and frenzied, like a war cry. "You see him yet?" he shouted. From the

A-framed roof, twigs and leafs slid to the ground, several chickens flapped through the small, oblong entry. The raccoon followed. Amid its black mask, beady eyes shone wet and wide. It scampered down the wood plank and darted after the slowest hen, lashing out with nimble claws, snarling like a mad dog.

"He's out, Pa!" Uriah tried to steady, but he shuddered hard—the rifle's stock struck his cheekbone. Then the throbbing made his eyes blur; to wipe them, he lowered the gun a second time. When they cleared, he saw his father, looming over him, his hairy arms across his thick chest. Uriah marked the disappointment on his face. Now Uriah knew he couldn't shoot, and from the crestfallen look in his father's steely eyes, he knew too. Frustration overtook Uriah, and he began to cry. He hid his face in the crook of his elbow.

Uriah's father ripped the rifle from his grasp, dropped to one knee and tilted his head toward his shoulder—the rifle balanced between. He plucked back the hammer and fired. The blast echoed through the farmlands, cleaving the ordinary stillness. Uriah lowered his arm from his eyes to see the creature wriggle and twitch, clicking savagely, then mewl like a newborn. Its gray-brown fur darkened as the blood issued forth. Then it jarred. Beside it, the mauled hen lay listless.

Uriah stood still as his father picked up his fallen hat— the curling brim and dusty ribbon tight against the crown— and plopped it atop his head. Uriah studied his father's face, watched the aspiration drain from his eyes, pulling down his pride, too. His father veered left, toward the barn, the sun's rays rich and full across his back. Calling over his shoulder, he said, "Bury 'em both. Put some gloves on first." His voice flat, wooden.

"Yes, sir."

Before his father disappeared, Uriah called after him, "You walkin' the perimeter this morning?"

"Not today, boy."

"Alright, Pa." Uriah tried to sound stolid. He donned his own hat—much less worn—and lumbered to the house for his gloves. He saw his mother duck from the window, and his heart sunk further. *She saw my cold feet,* he thought, then skulked inside.

"What's all the commotion out there?" his mother called from the kitchen.

"It's nothing, Ma. Just a coon. Pa took care of it." *God bless her, at least she pretends.*

"Pesky things. Wished they'd all jump into Lake Superior, drop like rocks."

Uriah knew she wasn't speaking of him but couldn't help but wonder if maybe she sort of was, accidental like. He retrieved his gloves from the highboy and crept passed her.

Outside, Uriah bent over the animals, the raccoon's eyes big and burnishing like marbles and its coat slippery and matted. He picked up the wounded hen by its yolk-yellow feet, the toes like rubber. Its white plumage was spattered red, the feathers coarse and tousled. Then it gave a little lurch, and Uriah did, too.

"She ain't dead," he said aloud and walked across the yard, down the slope that led to the cabbage patch, beyond the house and barn. "This is a private thing." He spoke as if the hen understood the circumstance. "No one needs to see."

He laid the bleeding bird in a sedgy stretch, its thin head perked upward. Tears formed, but he would not let them fall. Not for pride's sake but rather the dignity of the bird. He wanted to scream out to his father, to everyone, "My strength is big! You just don't see it."

He reared the shovel high in front of him, arms bent out in triangles. The hen peered into his eyes. Light glinted off the shovel's metal tip. "God, just one fell swoop, please," he whispered. He sucked in through his nose, fast and hard, then thrust downward with all his might.

Uriah dug a shallow grave for the lifeless fowl, laid it in slow then stroked its crimped feathers once. He patted down the stirred up earth and covered it with ryegrass and thistle. With his chin resting on the shovel's handle, he said, "I'm not too sure about prayers for a chicken. I only know 'em for people."

Clearing his throat, Uriah recited, "God our Father, Your power brings us to birth. You guide our lives, and by Your command, we return to dust." He paused, made the sign of the cross over the mound of dirt and weeds. In the distance, something caught his attention. It was Pa, strolling the perimeter. Dropping his head, Uriah breathed in the ripe, fresh smell of autumn and the tinny scent of blood, wondering if he'd ever be the same.

unfolded

"Yes, sir." I scoot my chair forward, not closer, just forward, and the wooden legs cheep against the floor. Instead of at his hip, I'm sitting just beneath his shoulder. *No farther though,* I tell myself. *Keep some distance, from his face, his gaze, his indifference.* Against the sterile white sheets, his skin looks gray. I try not to feel anything: no sadness, no anger, no love; yet I feel all three, welled up and perched in my throat. I stare at the worn wallpaper above his head—fat, vertical columns, gold then yellow, then gold. The hush feels clumsy. I think, *This cannot be comforting to him? Can it?* But if rigid, thick silence is all a dying man wants, well, who am I not to oblige?

"Son." The word sounds like he put it through a colander, low and strained. And difficult to bare. In response, I simply tighten my cheeks and forehead and lean in a little. He raises his bony fingers and spans them out. For me to hold, I presume. But I let them hover. So he drops his hand on the bed and says, "Talk to me."

I can feel my face slacken. And the blood rush begins, pulsing hard, then harder. Below his knobby knuckle sits a heart monitor, the light is a dull, sickly red. I hope that it starts spinning or flickering. Or whatever. Just fill this big, ugly white space. *Say something,* I command myself. *Fuck, say anything.* We speak, at the same time:

"I don't know what to—"

"How are the—"

Then we wait for one another to continue. My chest feels

light and my heart skittish, like when you're about to run a race and the starter's gun is up. This is it. I'm going to tell him. I'm going to say, "You hurt me, Dad." And by God, he's going to hear me.

"Please, boy, you go," he says, then exhales, heavy. His lips are thin and stuck together in the corners. I look between my knees and study the tile a moment—it's old but polished, with random black specks. I think they look like ants. I suck in hard through my nostrils, let my mouth bunch to one side, a half smile, and lift my head. His stare is iced over now and blank.

When I open my mouth, his eyes idle, then, slow as pouring oil, they close.

a bicycle for Madeline

It's 3:15, time for the ice cream truck. Madeline springs from the sofa. The taut plastic cover shifts and crinkles. She levels out the creases with both hands, first one way, then the other. After taking a step back to inspect for hints of any hidden folds, she bites at her thumbnail and moves in for another tug—here, there. Then she starts over. "Pa rum pum," she says, tapping the arm of the couch three times with her pointer finger. After the final credits roll, she clicks off her soap opera and beelines for the big picture-frame window.

Amidst the comfort of central-air, she imagines the humidity outside, how it would feel against her skin, in her hair. She ponders its tastelessness and its density on her tongue, like sticky cotton. To her, the city streets look wet, draped with the heavy June air. The heart of the urban center seems hardly moving, its blood beating thick as syrup. Softening the wail of sirens and low droning traffic is the faint laughter of children playing in the courtyard below. The youngsters' joy ignites a familiar, unwelcome ache in Madeline's womb—a longing for the little ones she'll never have. In her mind's eye, there's a boy and a girl, running to her, through a vast field of ripe, nutty grain. Their arms are spanned wide, reaching out. And she's reaching too. Then, she watches as they slam into her windowpane, their necks jolting and their bodies bouncing backward. Her arms still extended. The faceless children look past her, into the loneliness of her apartment; their faces wrench as if they've bitten lemons. They turn to one another, to her, their eyes slippery and bewildered. As they saunter away, the sky opens up. And warm, gray rain issues forth with round, full drops, as if poured from a watering can. The children gambol in the cloudburst, holding onto one another and never looking back.

"Change your thoughts, Madeline," she says aloud, shuddering some. And when she peels back the curtain, a vertical beam of light cuts through the parlor like a slice of cake, thin at first, then wider. "It's Tuesday," she says, "Music Box Dancer day." At first, the chimes of the white and yellow striped truck sound like a sparrow's warble, and Madeline smiles fully, humming the notes, wondering what a music box has to do with ice cream. But as the bright swirled cones painted on the truck's side come into view and the sound draws near, Madeline's mouth tightens, forming into a straight line across her jawline. The trilling chimes hollow out, into a mechanical echo. She pulls at a black tuft of hair dangling over her temple. "Oh, God." She pushes her ear against the pane till it flattens. "That's Turkey in the Straw. Oh no. No, no, no, no, no. It's Tuesday. Fuck. It's Music Box Dancer day." Panic wells, and the acid crawls up her throat. Spinning on her heel, she trips over a neatly angled pile of sheet music. But the tune grows louder before she can get to the bedroom. "No, no, no!" she cries out, jerking wisps of hair from her sloe, patchy mane. The urge to leap from her body swells as the girthy snake reappears, slinking over her feet and up her legs, its scales oily and damp. It slides farther up, flicking its clammy tongue, but her feet are moored. Her vocal cords severed. "Think of other things," she says, over and over, then slaps her hands over her ears.

"The bike!" *Look at your bike*, she thinks. *That'll balance things.* She steps to the bedroom window and lifts the middle two blinds with her eyes pressed shut. When she pops open her eyes, an exhale escapes through pursed lips, for in the slender iron bars of an otherwise empty rack leans a mossy green bicycle. "Just one more day," she whispers. Through the faux wood slats, she studies her bike a long while. The loopy drop bars like a ram, head down, readying to butt and batter. Its worn wheels and perpendicular storage rack—the chrome flaking away like chapped skin. "My beautiful bicycle," she says, sucking in quickly, then breathing out, "And my nemesis." She reviews the plan in her head once more. Thirty-six steps—medium pace—to the exit. Twenty-one from the door to the tenement gardens, then four more to the bike rack. In exhausting detail, she envisions the path, from the beige bead-board in the corridor to the dank stairwell. To the possible sounds—yipping dogs, car horns, and the wind through the Sugarberry trees that line the banks of a nearby brook—shrouded by the urban sprawl. Or so she imagines. To the mix of city smells—garbage, distant hydrangeas, and dog shit. As she anticipates, her nerves began to fire, low voltage. "Control your breathing," she says. "Like the doctor says, in through the nose, out through the mouth." In, out. Still, her brain whirs. And she rushes to the foyer, for her cello. Atop the instrument is a post-it note, blue and crisp, it reads, "Change Your Thoughts." Madeline pulls it from the instrument and taps its bridge three times. "Pa rum pum."

Madeline grips her cello like a hammer with one hand. With the other, she strokes the glassy wood, fingers the

F-holes. She positions the end in the space between her legs, then closes her eyes, tilts back her head. The bow is no longer a tool but a captive. And on this night, the eve before her re-acquaintance with the world, Madeline makes love. Her slender fingers caress and fondle the strings. And as she performs, she weeps, from the depths of her belly. She plays for fear. She plays for regret, at having vowed to leave her apartment. She thinks of her bicycle, calls it forlorn, then plays for that too. Her fist is clutched, knuckles white as eggshells, and she skids across the four strands. The horse-hair is hot to the touch, sounding her lament—raw, deep, and rich. "How did you come to this?" she says. "A covenant… with a damn bike?" Then she strums more wildly, for her stepfather with his lazy eye and buttery smile. And she plucks away, for the too small tent and his special camping trips.

Madeline plays with abandon till her fingers are stiff, her back wet—an inkblot test forming on her terry cloth shirt. "Just nine flights, Madeline," she says, "sixty-one stairs." She sits in silence, watching herself mount the three-speed Huffy. Her panting planes off. And the urge to pray sneaks in. She hasn't petitioned God in years, not since the boys from 6-B chose her to terrorize and mock. For a moment, she recalls the horrors—masturbation noises through her door each night, snorting like feral animals, calling out her name; smeared shit on her knob, in the grooves of her gold-plaited numbers; and cigarette smoke blown beneath her door. *Not sure I should be talking to you, God*, she muses. *You don't seem particularly interested in my grief.* But she laces her fingers together, pushes them against her forehead. "Give me strength tomorrow, God. Let me get past this threshold. Let me sit on my bike. Please. You owe me that." She makes the sign of the cross, slow and clumsy, slumping down next to the cello.

Her mind drifts to a lighter time. To the first time she asked the black-eyed delivery boy to count his strides coming and going from the elevator. He twisted up his face, palmed his downy hair. "Describe the hallway to me, too," she had asked. "And take the stairs instead of the elevator some time, Saul. Tell me how they smell. How they feel."

"Pardon, ma'am?"

"You heard me, this door is thin. And why not? You could use the exercise. Or maybe the peephole adds some pounds." She remembers his laugh, low and hearty, and his grimace, crooked—handsomely so—and honest. The college-bound lad warmed up to Madeline, and she holds that close. He handed back the sarcasm, two-fold. "Miss your Agoraphobics meeting again?" he'd ask. Or, "You know there's a cure, you mole. It's called weed." Madeline tried to keep her distance. *He's moving away*, she told herself over and over. But she knew that, to Saul, she was more than the crazy lady in 10-B.

"How many steps today?" she'd ask.

"The same."

Then she'd slide the envelope under the doorframe, and think, *Please don't leave me, Saul*. "Pa rum pum," and tap the door. Through the tiny round hole, Madeline always watched Saul walk away. And after he had gone, she would look both ways, once, twice, three times, then pull in the groceries, quick like a scampering squirrel. Her heart broke, every time, as she trudged to the calendar and marked it off in red. *Seven days till he returns.*

Before Saul left for college, on his last delivery, Madeline double-checked the chain locks—the night before and the morning of. Scared of missing his approach, she stood for an hour, pushed against the door, her body, her face, her hands. When he finally materialized, her heart raced, but she managed to sliver the door open and poke an envelope through. "It won't fit under the door," she spat. "Believe me, I've tried." She grabbed her trembling wrist with her free hand. "It's a little something extra, you know, for college."

"Ma'am, I can't—"

She cut him off, flapping it about. "Take it, you pain-in-the-ass. Hurry up. You know how nutty I can get."

Saul culled the money from her hand, and Madeline watched herself close the door, heavily, then rest against it. She heard his guttural voice again. "Pa rum pum," he whispered. Then gave her three soft taps from the other side.

Amidst the summoning, Madeline had avoided tomorrow's risky pilgrimage for a moment. But now, she looks through the crystal clear pane and peers out at her bike, its reflectors glinting in the yellowy autumn sun. Pelted by the wet seasons and having baked beneath the red rage of many Indian summers, the Huffy is still beautiful to Madeline. Her innards churn for its aloneness. "I'll be strong, for you," she says, letting go of the string at the window's edge. Fatigued by the day's broken routines, Madeline's gait is slow, her head and heart are weighty. "It's Tuesday," she mutters. "Music Box Dancer day."

Madeline hears the mourning doves calling out their

names. Her chest constricts. *Now or never*, she thinks. And after dressing in the clothes she chose months before—dark blue skirt, just above the knee, a light gray, long sleeve, nylon T-shirt, white sneakers, and finally, a Detroit Tigers baseball cap, pulled down over her brow—she makes her way. *I don't feel real. Just don't stop*, she tells herself, *and stay in autopilot, so you can't turn back.* Unlocking all of the latches and bolts, she forces herself to think about the ice cream truck, then whips open the door. She gasps at a swoosh of warm air, tepid and thick, like chicken soup. As planned, she sticks her foot between the frame and hardwood, keeping the door ajar, then mimes her way into the hall. With her hands and legs splayed out, she keeps her face to the wall, inching like a caterpillar. Half a step, then another. And another.

Stop.

In all the preparation for this day, Madeline never thought about a cable-man showing up—or anyone for that matter— as she flounders in the hall amidst her own shadow. Yet here he comes, striding closer, then closer. She stands still, a part of the wall, like broken sheetrock. With her cheek pressed to the wall, she can only see him with one eye. A broad-chested fellow, bearded and ungainly. Even with his cell phone cocked between his shoulder and ear and scribbling madly on a crumpled piece of paper resting in his palm, he takes notice of her. Madeline's face flushes hot, and there's a pang in her bladder. She twitches at the sharpness. The burly man with the bright white nametag passes by, peering at her from his periphery. Then he looks forward again and continues talking, pretending not to see.

The acid travels up her throat, burning her lips and gums.

She pounds her fists against the drywall. And the snake begins to slither up her fine blue skirt.

As the sun goes down, Madeline stays crouched in the hallway, three feet from her apartment, legs tucked beneath her, aching from the hours of stillness. Another bout of urine spills onto the carpet, darkening the wide circle around her. Her plucked out hair is strewn about the floor, some strands still caught in her fingers, others fixed in the stale piss, forked out like frayed crochet.

After the policeman maneuvers her back inside and the doctor on call from the Skyland Psychiatry Clinic has gone, Madeline sits like stone upon the plastic slipcover. When the bicycle cries out to her, she snatches up her cello. Even amidst her angry concerto, she can still hear it wailing.

"You lied!"

She plays more frantically.

"You're a coward!"

Madeline draws the curtains across the window in one fell swoop and strides to the calendar. Without pause, she takes it down off the wall. "Pa rum pum," she says, tapping the barren and discolored space. Her hue is silvery, full-blooded. And she hunkers down on the floor again, next to her cello. "Thank you, God. For the certainty, I mean." With her sleeve, she buffs out a fingerprint on the glossy cello then stands the bow upright. Then, she carefully positions the calendar under the instrument's endpin, like a towel. "No blood on the carpet, Madeline." As she drags her slight wrists down the coarse strings, she exhales, breathy, tired and composed.

acknowledgements

- "The Day the Guinea Pigs Went Missing" (revised) – shortlisted by *F(r)iction Magazine,* 2017 and published by *Broken Ribbon,* sponsored by Killer Nashville.
- "Uriah's Last Rite" (revised) – winner of the 2017 Adobe Cottage Writer's Retreat
- "unfolded" – runner-up in *Exposition Review's* Flash 405 contest, 2017
- "a bicycle for Madeline" – winner of the Rusty Scythe Prize Book award, 2016 and Semi-Finalist in the 2017 Cinematic Short Story Contest by *ScreenCraft.*

To the following, my heartiest gratitude: Suzanne, Roger and Joshua Broughman; Zach Meadows, Kylie Seitz, Liz Whiteacre, and the entire staff at Etchings Press, as well as the University of Indianapolis; Eric Forrest at Rusty Scythe Publishing; staff of Broken Ribbon via Killer Nashville; Sara Roberts and Barbara Seidl at Café Aphra: On-line Community of Writers; John Mauk, Nancy Parshall and the rest of the family at Interlochen College of Creative Arts; Robin Lippincott, Scott O'Connor, Kellie Carle and Lindsay Zibach, among other special friends from Spalding University's MFA program; Susan Donovan at Adobe Cottage Writer's Retreat; Lalo Vasquez; Chris Harris; Thom Blanck; Jan McDonald; Dixie Hankinson; and Sandy and Charlotte Sanford.

Above all, my extraordinary family: Erin, Gray and Hudson.

colophon

The cover and title texts are set in American Typewriter.
The body text is set in STIXGeneral.

author biography

After a southern Michigan childhood, Chad V. Broughman worked for a brief stint in the banking industry throughout the state of Georgia then pursued a career in education. He is a prose writer and English/Creative Writing teacher living in Harbor Springs, Michigan, a scenic resort community on the northern shores of Lake Michigan. Chad won the 2016 Rusty Scythe Prize Book award and has been published in numerous reviews and journals nationwide—such as *Carrier Pigeon, East Coast Literary Review, River Poets Journal,* and *Burningword*—and is forthcoming in Killer Nashville's *Broken Ribbon.* As well, he won the 2017 Adobe Cottage Writers Retreat in New Mexico and, most recently, was named a finalist in the William Faulkner: William Wisdom Creative Writing Competition and earned a certificate of Distinction from New Millennium Writings. Chad holds an MFA from Spalding University and co-edits the online fiction/poetry blog, *Café Aphra,* based in the United Kingdom. All that said, Chad is most proud of his role as a family man—father to his two rambunctious young boys, Gray and Hudson, and husband to his forbearing wife, Erin.

Etchings Press

Etchings Press is a student-run publisher at the University of Indianapolis. Each year, student editors choose the Whirling Prize, a post-publication award, in the fall and coordinate a publication contest for one poetry chapbook, one prose chapbook, and one novella in the spring. For more information, please visit etchings.uindy.edu.

Previous winners and publications

Poetry
2019: *As Lovers Always Do* by Marne Wilson
2018: *In the Herald of Improbable Misfortunes* by Robert Campbell
2017: *Uncle Harold's Maxwell House Haggadah* by Danny Caine
2016: *Some Animals* by Kelli Allen
2015: *Velocity of Slugs* by Joey Connelly
2014: *Action at a Distance* by Christopher Petruccelli

Prose
2019: *Dissenting Opinion from the Committee for the Beatitudes*
        by Marc J. Sheehan (fiction)
2018: *The Forsaken* by Chad V. Broughman (fiction)
2017: *Unravelings* by Sarah Cheshire (memoir)
2016: *Pathetic* by Shannon McLeod (essays)
2015: *Ologies* by Chelsea Biondolillo (essays)
2014: *Static: Stories* by Frederick Pelzer (fiction)

Novella
2019: *Savonne, Not Vonny* by Robin Lee Lovelace
2018: *Edge of the Known Bus Line* by James R. Gapinski
2017: *The Denialist's Almanac of American Plague and
        Pestilence* by Christopher Mohar
2016: *Followers* by Adam Fleming Petty